Heart of the Country